The Strange Museum:
The Midnight Ride

Strange Family Home

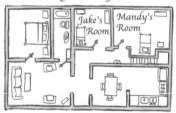

Jake's Room

Mandy's Room

2nd Floor

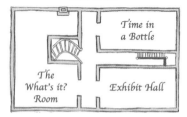

The What's it? Room

Time in a Bottle

Exhibit Hall

1st Floor

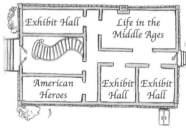

Exhibit Hall

Life in the Middle Ages

American Heroes

Exhibit Hall

Exhibit Hall

Basement

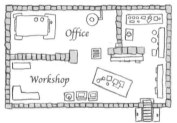

Office

Workshop

STRANGE MUSEUM

The Strange Museum

STRANGE MUSEUM

The Midnight Ride

Written by
Jahnna N. Malcolm

Illustrated by
Sally Wern Comport

ISBN 1-933863-37-4

10 9 8 7 6 5 4 3 2 1

Listen, my children, and you shall hear
Of the midnight ride of Paul Revere,
On the 18th of April, in '75;
Hardly a man is now alive
Who remembers that famous day and year.

—Henry Wadsworth Longfellow

Contents

Chapter One
Meet the Strange Family

Jake and Mandy hated their last name. *Strange.* They were normal kids, but people always called them "those Strange children" from "that Strange family."

"We might as well be named the Weirdos," Jake said. "Because that's what all the guys in 6th grade call us."

Mandy agreed. Friends at school had always made fun of her last name. Now that she was in

8th grade, the teasing seemed to be worse. "I wish Mom and Dad had normal jobs," she said. "Why did they have to open a museum?"

"That would be fine with me," Jake said. "But did they have to call it the *Strange* Museum? Bad idea!"

Their parents, Kate and Ben Strange, used to work at an arts and science museum. That was how they met. They had always dreamed of owning their own museum. Not a big museum. A small one, with very rare objects in it.

A year ago, Mr. and Mrs. Strange saw a For Sale sign in front of the big stone home on Front Street. It was the oldest home in town. No one had lived there for years. People said there were ghosts in it. Mr. and Mrs. Strange thought it was perfect. They could open a museum on the first and second floors. Their family would live on the top floor.

The Strange Museum was not an art
museum. And it was not a science museum. Oh, it
had paintings and it had test tubes, and things like
that. But everything in the Strange Museum was

picked because of an odd story that went with it. It was a museum filled with lost and found objects from around the world. So they called it the Strange Museum of Lost and Found.

Three days a week, Jake and Mandy helped their mom and dad after school. As soon as they got home, they put on blue T-shirts with the Strange Museum printed on the pocket. It was their job to tell people about the objects in their museum. Sometimes they showed children the bathrooms. And other times they gave old people cups of water. Then, at five o'clock, they told people it was time to go home. When everyone was gone, they shut and locked the doors.

Jake and Mandy liked working in the museum. There were five rooms on the main floor and three rooms on the second floor. All of the rooms had strange names.

Jake loved the What's It? room. It was filled

with all sorts of odd things. Some were small enough to hold in your hand. Others were big wood boxes with moving parts. It was called the What's It? room because you had to guess what each thing did.

Mandy liked the Time in a Bottle room. Each bottle had something inside it. Some had little boats with flags and sails. Others had little

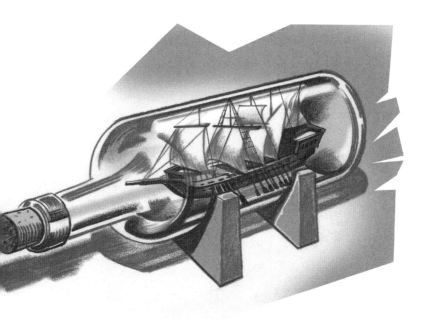

houses. Then there were the bottles with notes inside them. Mandy wished she could pull out all the notes and read them.

Jake and Mandy liked hearing the tale that went with each object. New things came into the museum every day, so there was always something fun to talk about.

On the days Jake worked in the museum, he felt great, but not today. Today Jake had an odd feeling. A scared feeling. Like something was going to happen at the museum. It made his insides do flip-flops.

That is why he took the long way home after school.

When Jake got to the museum, his sister was standing on the sidewalk in front of the big stone home. She was looking up. A red, white, and blue banner was stretched above the door. It read American Heroes.

The American Heroes room was the museum's newest exhibit. Their mom and dad had worked on it for months. It had lost and found objects that used to belong to famous Americans. There was a buckle from a Pilgrim's shoe. One of George Washington's socks was on display. It even had a speech that President Lincoln wrote.

Mandy turned her head to the side. Her straight dark hair fell across her shoulder.

"What are you doing out here?" Jake asked.

"Thinking," she said, as she looked up at the museum.

Jake set down his backpack and stood next to his sister. He was shorter than Mandy but looked a lot like her. Both had thick dark hair. Both had very blue eyes. "What are you thinking about?" he asked.

Mandy kept looking up as she talked. "If this

really is a museum of lost and found objects, then someone must have lost them. And that person is still missing them."

Jake was confused. "Where? Back in time?"

"Well, yes," Mandy said. "George Washington is probably looking everywhere for his sock. And President Lincoln is going from room to room in the White House looking for his speech."

Jake stared at his sister. Sometimes she came up with pretty strange ideas. But this one was a whopper. He made up his mind to play along with her.

"What about that map in the American Heroes room?" he said. "Who do you think is looking for that?"

The map didn't have a name on it. Mr. and Mrs. Strange had put clues on a big poster above the map. The poster said the map was from 1775. It said a very important man used it. The poster also said it was only used once. Children were asked to guess whose map it was.

"That map is too weird for words," Mandy said. "The other day, I was up there alone. I thought I would try to get a close look at the map. So I opened the glass case."

"Hey! Mom and Dad said not to do that!" Jake said. Their parents were very strict about the rules. No one was ever to touch an object in the museum.

Mandy rolled her eyes. "I *know* that. But I couldn't help it. So I opened the glass case."

"And?" Jake said.

Mandy made a face at her brother. "I don't think I should tell you."

"Tell me!" Jake barked. "Or I'll tell Mom you opened the case."

"OK." Mandy spoke in a very low voice. She looked behind her to make sure no one else could hear. "I put my hand out to touch the map and the room started to spin."

Jake felt the little hairs on his neck stand up. "Go on," he whispered.

"Then I heard a voice shouting."

"From where?" Jake asked. "Outside the window?"

"No." Mandy looked her brother right in the eye. "From inside the map."

Chapter Two
The Map

Jake wanted to see the map. Jake wanted to hear the map. He wanted to find out if his sister was telling the truth.

Jake changed into his blue T-shirt as fast as he could. Then he ran to the museum lobby. Mandy did the same. They were about to go up the stairs when they heard their mom's voice behind them.

"There you two are!"

Mrs. Strange walked across the lobby toward the kids. She wore a white lab coat over a dark blue skirt. Her red hair was pulled into a bun on top of her head. It was held in place by a pencil and a magnifying glass. "We have a group from the America Club," she said. "They want a tour of our American Heroes room." She gave her children a warm smile. "I said you two would be glad to take them around."

Jake and Mandy looked at each other. They would have to wait to look at the map.

Lucky for the kids, the tour was lots of fun. The people knew a lot about the objects in the museum. They got very excited when they saw the pair of glasses that were Ben Franklin's.

"You know, Ben Franklin was not just a Founding Father of our country," one of the men said. "He was also a poet and an inventor. He probably made those very glasses."

"And somewhere in time, Ben is looking for them," Mandy whispered to Jake.

Jake smiled and added, "But he can't see to find them."

Before they knew it, it was almost five o'clock. A bell rang and their mother's voice came over the loudspeaker. "The museum will close in ten minutes. Ten minutes."

Mandy and Jake led their tour to the front door and waved good-bye. As they closed the door, their dad came up from the basement. He wore a pair of thick glasses and a small flashlight on a headband. That meant he had been in his workshop. He must have been fixing one of the objects from the museum."

"Hi, you two!" Dr. Strange called. "Will you close up for me? Your mom and I have to go to a meeting. We don't want to be late."

"Sure, Dad," Jake replied.

"Remember to lock the doors and come right upstairs," Dr. Strange added as he ran up the stairs. "And please, don't touch a thing! Everything must stay just the way it is."

Jake locked the front doors. Mandy got a flashlight and turned off all the lights on the first floor. Then they turned to face each other. It was Jake who spoke first.

"Let's go see that map!"

They raced up the stairs to the American Heroes room at the far side of the museum. A flag with 13 stars hung over the big clock. There were 10 glass cases in the room and pictures on the walls. Mandy shone the flashlight on the map case.

Jake tiptoed up to the case. Mandy was right behind him.

"I have a funny feeling about this," Mandy said as they got closer to the map. "Maybe we should just go."

"Come on, Mandy," Jake said. "What are you, chicken?"

Mandy thought about it. "Yes, I am chicken. And you should be, too. I told you what happened before."

Jake did not hear her. He was staring at the map. It was drawn in black ink on a yellow piece of paper. Some of it was missing. But Jake could clearly see a handprint across one part. That handprint was more than two-hundred years old!

There were words on the map, but Jake couldn't make them out. Were they the names of towns? He lifted the glass to get a closer look.

"Jake!" Mandy warned. "Dad just said not to touch a thing."

Jake waved her off with his hand. "Dad said not to touch things that can break. This is just a piece of paper."

"It's more than that," Mandy said. "It's a

very old piece of paper from the 1700s. And it belonged to someone who was very important to America."

"You touched it. Why can't I?" Jake said as he reached for the map.

All of a sudden the room began to spin. Jake fell onto the map. Lights flashed. Jake heard a rush of wind in his ears. It got louder and louder.

"Jake! Where are you?" Mandy cried as the room became a blur.

Jake grabbed his sister's hand and closed his eyes. "Hold on!"

Chapter Three

Somewhere in Time

When Jake and Mandy opened their eyes, everything had changed. They were no longer in the museum. In fact, they were no longer in their town. They were standing in the middle of a dirt road somewhere out in the country. And it was dark.

"Am I dead?" Mandy asked Jake, who still held the map in his hand.

"If you are, then I am, too," Jake replied.

"Do I look dead?"

"No." Mandy spun in a slow circle and looked around her. Thick rows of trees lined both sides of the dirt road. There were no streetlights, just moonlight. "What happened? Where are we?"

"I don't know." Jake bent over and felt the road. He picked up a dirt clod and tossed it into the trees. The rattle of the clod against the leaves was very loud in the stillness. "Did you hear that?" Jake asked.

"Of course," Mandy said. "Why?"

"Can you feel this?" Jake pinched her arm.

"Ow!" Mandy yelled. "That hurt!"

Jake shrugged. "Then this isn't a dream."

"No. It's a nightmare," Mandy replied. "How did we get here? Where's our home?" Mandy could feel her chin start to shake. She felt like any second she was going to cry. "And where are Mom and Dad?"

Jake was as upset as his sister. He leaned his head back and called, "Mom! Dad! Where are you?"

Mandy joined him, shouting as loud as she could. "Help! Mom! Come get us!"

But there was no reply. All they heard was the sound of crickets in the night.

Mandy paced back and forth. "I don't like this. I don't like this one bit."

Jake started to talk really fast. "Maybe something exploded in the museum. And we were thrown into the air. Then a big wind blew us here. Maybe Mom and Dad are in their car looking for us. And maybe—"

"Shh!" Mandy put her hand over his mouth. "Do you hear that?"

There was a sound off in the trees.

"Is it a car?" Jake asked from behind her hand.

"No," Mandy cocked her head. "Something else."

Ker-thump. Ker-thump. Ker-thump.

The kids peered into the dark to see what was coming. The sound got louder and louder.

Then Jake's eyes grew wide. "I know what that is!" he cried. "It's a—"

"Horse!" Mandy screamed as a black horse and rider exploded out of the dark. The horse jumped over a low stone wall onto the road.

Before Jake and Mandy could get out of the way, the horse reared. The rider shouted and then fell backwards. He hit the ground with a loud thud.

The horse bolted into the trees and was gone. But the man did not move. He lay flat on his back, his arms out to his sides.

"Oh, no!" Jake cried as he ran to the man. "He's dead!"

Chapter Four
Man on the Road

Mandy bent over the man on the ground. She saw his chest move up and down. "He's not dead," she said. "He's knocked out. He must have hit his head."

"Thank goodness!" Jake sank to the ground. "I thought he was toast."

Mandy didn't hear her brother. She was too busy looking at the man's strange clothes. They looked like a costume. He wore a dark cape. His hat was made of wool and had three sides to it. He wore a long blue coat with brass buttons. His pants stopped at his knees. He wore long black boots.

"This guy looks like George Washington," Mandy said. "Except he doesn't have that big white wig. Is someone in town doing a play?"

Jake came up beside his sister. He bent down to look at the man. The hair on the back of his neck stood up again. "These clothes are real, Mandy," Jake said. "See? His boots have mud on them. And he has spurs."

"And his gloves are worn," Mandy said, carefully picking up one hand.

"We need to call a doctor." Jake tried to see if there was any blood on the man's head. It was hard to tell. The man's long dark hair was pulled back in a ponytail.

Mandy stood up and walked down the road. She was still holding the flashlight from the

museum. She flicked it on and aimed it into the trees. "I wonder if there is a house around here. Or a phone booth. We need to call 9-1-1." She turned back to her brother. "Check his bag. Maybe he has a cell phone."

Jake looked inside the brown bag that had fallen from the man's shoulder. He found a cloth bag of coins, a feather pen, and a leather bag. It had a stopper on it made of bone. The bag felt like it was full of water. "Boy, if he's an actor in a play, he has really gotten his part down," Jake called.

"You should see this stuff, Mandy. Everything in here looks like it's at least a hundred years old. Even the money is weird."

"Keep looking." Mandy shone the beam of light on the fields. "I don't see a house or light anywhere. I think it's going to be a long time before we see a car."

Jake looked hard at a torn piece of paper in the man's hand.

"Did you hear me, Jake?" Mandy called again.

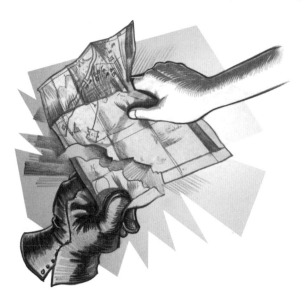

"I don't know when we'll ever see a car."

Jake held up the map he'd taken from the museum. He put it next to the paper in the man's hand. They made a perfect fit. "Try never," he said.

"Oh, Jake!" Mandy said, putting one hand on her hips. "You *always* look on the down side of things."

Jake couldn't stop staring at the map. It wasn't so much the map that upset him. It was what was written on it. There was a date. Below that was a name. One he knew very well.

"Um, Mandy?" Jake called in a shaky voice. "I have some good news and some bad news."

"So tell me the good news," Mandy said.

"The good news is I know who this guy is."

"That is good." Mandy ran back to join Jake. "So what's the bad news?"

"The year is 1775." Jake looked up at his sister and gulped. "And this guy is Paul Revere."

Chapter Five
Save the Country!

Jake knew his bad news would upset Mandy. But he had no idea it would make her pass out. But that's just what she did. Now he had *two* people passed out on the road. He ran to look in Paul Revere's bag. Inside it was the leather bag full of water.

Jake pulled out the stopper and took a sip. Then he put a little water on his sister's lips. Mandy sat up and rubbed her head.

"Tell me you were kidding," she said. "Did you really say this is 1775?"

Jake nodded. "Don't ask me how it could happen. All I know is that I touched this map and the room spun around. And then we were here." Jake held up the torn map. "The missing corner of this map is in Paul Revere's hand. He must have lost this part on his ride."

"Jake!" Mandy stared at her brother. "Are you telling me that this man lost that map over two-hundred years ago? And our museum found it? And when you put your hand on the map we were sent back in time?"

Jake shut one eye. "Well, um . . . yes."

"But why?" Mandy shouted.

Jake shrugged. "To help Paul Revere, I guess. Remember, he has to make that ride."

"What ride?"

"The midnight ride of Paul Revere," Jake

said. "Don't you know the poem? We had to learn it in English class." Jake put one hand on his chest and said,

> *"Listen, my children, and you shall hear*
> *Of the midnight ride of Paul Revere,*
> *On the 18th of April, in '75;*
> *Hardly a man is now alive*
> *Who remembers that famous day and year."*

When Jake was done, Mandy said, "I think I missed that day."

Jake put his hands on his hips. "Paul Revere is a really famous guy," he said. "He helped America split from England and become the USA."

"He did?" Mandy looked down at the man in the dirt.

"You see, we wanted to become our own country. But the British wanted us to stay part of England. So the king sent troops to stop us." Jake pointed to Paul Revere. "It was Paul's job to tell all the towns when the British troops were coming. That way they were ready to fight back."

"Did he tell them?" Mandy asked.

"Yes. And the Americans won the war. And this country became the USA."

"Oh, right," Mandy said with the wave of her hand. "Now I remember."

Jake walked back and forth. "I think you and I have to make the ride. Paul can't. He's passed out on the road."

"But how are we going to make the ride if we don't have a horse?" Mandy asked.

Crack!

Something big moved in the dark about 20 feet from them. Mandy hopped behind Jake. "What is it, a bear?"

The big thing walked toward them. Jake began to giggle.

"What's so funny?" Mandy asked, punching

him in the back.

"That bear is a horse," Jake said.

Mandy peeked out from behind Jake and smiled. Paul Revere's horse plodded up to them. Its saddle was still on its back. A few feet behind it came two other horses. They did not have saddles.

"It looks like Paul's horse found some friends," Jake said.

The horses stood in the road a few feet away from the kids. Paul Revere's horse came forward and pressed its nose on Jake's arm.

"It's trying to tell you something," Mandy said. "I think it wants you to get on."

"Me?" Jake said. "What about you? You're the rider."

"I went to the Trails West Ranch for my birthday when I was ten," Mandy said. "That does *not* make me a rider."

"It makes you more of a rider than me," Jake shot back. "Did *I* get to go to the ranch? No. *I* had to have a skating party for my tenth birthday."

"Don't start that again," Mandy said as she took the horse by the reins. "I'll hold her, and you get on."

Jake crossed his arms. "I won't go unless you go. Besides, we don't even know *where* we are supposed to go."

"Yes, we do," Mandy said. "You have the map."

"I have *part* of the map," Jake said. "Paul Revere has the other part."

"Well, go get it. I'm sure we can figure it out."

Jake did not move.

Mandy stomped her foot. "Look! You're the one who said we came back in time for a reason.

You said we had to help Paul Revere tell the people about the troops that are coming. If we don't do it, our country may lose the war and never become the USA. And that would change everything. It may even erase us."

"Well, if you put it *that* way, then I will get the map." Jake ran over to Paul Revere, who still lay on his back in the road. Jake pulled apart the man's fingers and took the map.

As Jake stood up, a hand reached out and grabbed his arm.

"Yikes!" Jake yelled.

"What are you doing?" Paul Revere moaned. "Who are you?"

"Hello, Mr. Revere," Jake said. "I'm Jake and this is my sister, Mandy. We are here to help you warn people about the troops."

Paul Revere tried to sit up, but his head hurt too much. He flopped back on the ground. "How

do you know about that?"

Mandy moved next to him. "It's a long story. And we don't have much time."

Paul nodded. "No time. You two take my horse. And my map."

Jake nodded. Mandy held the horse while he put his foot in the stirrup and tried to get on. It took three tries, with Mandy pushing him on the bottom. Then Jake held out his hand, and Mandy swung onto the saddle behind him.

"Ow!" Mandy cried as she landed. "Scoot forward."

"I *am* forward," Jake said. "If I go any more, I'll fall off the horse."

"No, you won't." Mandy gave him a big shove and made some room for herself. Then she turned to Paul Revere. "What is your horse's name?"

"Brown Beauty," Paul Revere replied. "But

she's not my horse."

Jake patted the horse's back. "Good horse."

Paul Revere tried to sit up again. "Ride north to Lexington." He pointed down the road. "Tell them. Tell everyone."

Jake gave the horse a kick in the side. Brown Beauty sprang forward. Mandy held on to Jake. As they rode off, she shouted back, "What do we tell them?"

"The British are coming!"

Chapter Six

The Midnight Ride

Brown Beauty pounded down the dirt road. Jake held on for dear life. Mandy had her arms wrapped around his waist. Her head bumped into his back as the horse jogged them up and down.

"Mandy!" Jake called. "I think I see a home up ahead."

"Good! Tell the horse to stop."

"Stop, horse!" Jake yelled. "Stop!"

"Don't be silly," Mandy said. "Pull back on the reins and say *whoa!*"

"Look, if you want to drive, then *you* get in front," Jake shot back. "There is nothing to hang onto up here."

A brick home came up on their left. Mandy reached around her brother and pulled on the reins. "Whoa!"

The horse came to a stop. Mandy gave Jake her know-it-all smile. "See how easy that was?"

Jake did not reply. He took the flashlight from Mandy and looked at the map again. "This must be the Wilson farm," he said. "Do you want to tell them, or should I?"

All of a sudden Mandy got very still. "You do it. I don't know what to say."

Jake cupped his hand around his mouth. "The British are coming!" he shouted at the dark windows. "The British troops are coming!"

A light came on upstairs. A man came to the window. He held a candle in his hand. He looked down and waved.

"Hey, he heard us!" Mandy cried. "Isn't that cool?"

Jake smiled. "Totally cool."

Mandy looked at the map, then pointed up the road. "Lexington is that way. We have some more farms on the way."

"Then what are we waiting for?" Jake gave their horse a gentle kick. "Let's go, Beauty!"

The horse galloped down the road past farm after farm. At each home the children would yell, "The British are coming! The troops are coming!" Then a light would come on. Sometimes someone would call, "Thank you."

"Wow, this is like Halloween," Mandy said. "Only people don't give you candy."

"No, they give you thanks," Jake said,

"which is better."

At first Jake kept a firm hold of the reins. Then he began to relax. Even Mandy let go of her grip on Jake. Now she rode with just one arm about his middle.

They came around a bend in the road. "I wish this horse had headlights," Jake said. "These woods are so dark."

Mandy saw something move in the trees.

"Did you see that?" she hissed.

"See what?" Jake asked in a loud voice.

"Shh!" She put her finger to her lips. "Whatever is out there might hear us."

Mandy shone the flashlight at the movement. Two men stood under the trees on the side of the road. They wore red coats. Their horses were nearby.

Jake had seen pictures of British troops. They wore red coats. In fact, they were called 'redcoats.'

"Oh, my gosh!" Jake gasped. "It's them. The British!"

"Halt!" one of the men cried. "Who goes there?"

Mandy pointed her light at the man's eyes. He held his hands up to block the glare. The other man reached for his musket.

"What do we do now?" Jake said.

"Turn around!" Mandy hissed. "And RUN!"

Jake yanked the reins hard to the right. The horse turned and ran back the way they came.

"Stop! In the name of the king!" the other man shouted after them.

Mandy and Jake leaned forward to make the horse go faster. They heard shouts as the British got on their horses. Soon the sound of hoof beats pounded behind them.

"Where do we go?" Jake cried. His heart beat like a drum in his chest. He had never been

so scared in his life. "I don't know what to do!"

"Ask no questions!" a deep voice called from beside them. "And follow me!"

Chapter Seven
Run from the Redcoats!

Out of the dark came a man on a horse. He rode bareback. A dark cape hung from his shoulders. His hat was pushed back on his head. He had no bridle and held onto the horse's mane with his hands.

"It's Paul Revere!" Mandy cried.

The hoof beats grew closer. The shouts from the British grew louder. "Stop! Stop, I say!"

"This way!" Paul turned his horse to the

left. It leaped over a stone wall. "We'll try to lose those British redcoats."

"It's a jump!" Jake called to his sister. "Hold on!"

Mandy shut her eyes. Their horse sailed over the wall. Jake let go of the reins. He clung to the horse's neck and let it follow Paul Revere.

They pounded across the fields. The horses ran down hills and through the woods. The sounds behind them changed. Now only one horse was following them. Paul Revere made a sharp right turn. In the moonlight they saw he was headed for a big pond.

"Water!" Jake warned Mandy. "We may have to swim for it."

Just before Paul Revere got to the pond, he turned his horse and hid out of sight. Jake and Mandy followed. Their horses came to a stop, and Paul put his finger to his lips.

They dared not move. The redcoat came

closer and closer. Just as he rode to the edge of the pond, Paul kicked his horse. It leaped forward and scared the British redcoat's horse.

With a shout, the redcoat fell off his horse. He hit the water with a splash. His horse ran into the darkness.

Paul rode back to Jake and Mandy. "Now we ride as fast as we can," he said. "First to Lexington. Then on to Concord."

The hours ticked away as Jake and Mandy followed Paul Revere on his ride. It was midnight when they began. The moon was high in the sky then. Now it peeked out above the trees. They passed house after house. Sometimes Mandy called to the people inside. Sometimes it was Jake or Paul.

Their legs hurt. Their eyes burned from trying to see in the dark. But Jake and Mandy had never felt so alive. They were a part of history.

At last they came to the town of Lexington.
Paul Revere slowed his horse. The dirt road
became a cobblestone street. He led them to the

center of town. They stopped in front of a brick house with black shutters. They could see that some candles still burned inside.

A man with a gun stood in front of the door. "What do you want?"

"I am Paul Revere," he said. "Tell the men inside that I'm here."

"Be quiet, sir. The family has gone to bed," the man with the gun ordered. "You might wake them."

Paul Revere hopped off his horse. "Someone had better wake them. If we don't, the British will. The troops are on their way."

"What!" The man's eyes grew wide.

Paul Revere pushed him aside and beat on the door. "Get up! All of you!"

More lights came on. A man popped his head out of the window. "Oh, it's you, Paul. Come in! Come in!"

Mandy and Jake got off their horse. Their legs felt like jelly. They were tired. It had been a long night.

Paul Revere walked back to them. "I must go inside. There are men here who are trying to help our country. This is no place for children."

Mandy could not help being nosy. "What men?" she asked.

"They are all Sons of Liberty," he said.

Just hearing the word 'liberty' sent a chill up and down her arms.

She and Jake looked up at Paul Revere. It was the closest they had been to him since he fell off his horse. He cocked his head. He looked at Jake in his jeans and T-shirt. Then at Mandy, in her skirt and T-shirt. The kids knew they must look very strange.

"I do not know who you are or where you come from," Paul Revere said slowly. "But I must give you my thanks. Here is for your pains."

He placed a silver coin in Jake's hand.

"What's this for?" Jake asked. "We made you fall off your horse."

Paul shook his head. He pointed to the map Jake still had in his hand. "You found that map. If the British had gotten it first, we would all be doomed."

Jake smiled. "We're just glad to help."

Mandy jabbed her brother in the side.

"Ow!" Jake cried. "Why did you do that?"

"Give Mr. Revere his map," she said. "So he can finish his ride."

"Oh, right." Jake held out the paper. "Here's your map, sir."

Paul Revere took it. When his fingers touched the map, the world spun. Lights flashed.

"Oh, no!" Mandy grabbed Jake's hand. "Not again!"

Jake had just enough time to shout, "Good-bye, Mr. Revere. Good luck!"

Then they were gone.

Chapter Eight
Lost and Found

In a flash, Jake and Mandy were back in the Strange Museum. The flag with 13 stars was still on the wall. The display cases were still there.

Jake looked at the clock. No time had passed. He looked at his sister. Her eyes were wide. Her mouth hung open. She patted her face. She patted his face. Then she reached out to feel a chair.

"Don't touch a thing in this museum!" Jake said. "I want to stay here."

"Then it's true?" Mandy asked in a hushed voice. "We really did take a trip back in time?"

Jake nodded. "And we really met Paul Revere."

Mandy gulped. "And we really helped him warn the people about the British troops?"

"Yes, we did all that," Jake said. "But we can never prove it."

"What about the map?" Mandy asked.

They ran to look in the glass case. The top was open but the map was gone. So were the clues and the contest.

"Where's the map?" Mandy asked.

"I gave it to Paul Revere, remember?" Jake said.

Mandy snapped her fingers. "That's right. He lost the map. And we found it and gave it back to him."

"And now the map is no longer lost," Jake said. "Which is why it's not here."

Mandy spoke in a whisper. "Then we changed the future."

Jake bent over the glass case. "There's something else in the map's place."

Mandy shone the flashlight on the case. "Look, Jake, she said, "it's some old coins."

Jake pointed to the first row of coins. "There's a blank spot. One of the coins is missing."

"I wonder which one it is," Mandy said.

There were four rows of very old silver coins. They had pictures of kings on them.

Jake smiled and put his hand in his pocket. "I think I know." He held up a silver coin. It was the one Paul Revere gave to him. The date on it said 1775.

"Of course!" Mandy said. "But don't you want to keep that for yourself? Just to prove that we didn't dream this whole night."

"It would be cool to keep it," Jake said as he

put the coin in the empty spot. "But it would not prove that we went back in time. And it would not prove we met Paul Revere."

Mandy nodded. "I guess it will just have to be *our* secret."

Jake smiled. He liked secrets. And he didn't mind sharing this one with his sister.

"Let's get out of here," Mandy said, looking around the room, "before something else happens."

As they walked up to the top floor, the kids thought about their adventure. Something strange had sent them on a trip back in time. Would it happen again? Jake hoped so.

"Don't tell anyone," Jake said to Mandy. "But this really is a *Strange* museum."

Mandy grinned. "And we really are one *Strange* family!"

About the Authors

JAHNNA N. MALCOLM stands for Jahnna "and" Malcolm. Jahnna Beecham and Malcolm Hillgartner are married and have published over ninety books for kids and teens. They've written about ballerinas, horses, ghosts, singing cowboys, and green slime. Their most recent book series is called The Jewel Kingdom, and it is about adventurous princesses. They even made a movie of the first book in the series, *The Ruby Princess Runs Away*.

Before Jahnna and Malcolm wrote books, they were actors. They met on the stage and were married on the stage, and now they live in Oregon. They used to think of their ideas for their books by themselves. Now they get help from their son, Dash, and daughter, Skye.

About the Illustrator

SALLY WERN COMPORT'S illustrations have been seen nationally for over fifteen years. A 1976 graduate of Columbus College of Art & Design, she began her career as an art director at several agencies before beginning full-time illustration in 1983. Her work has received numerous honors including The Society of Illustrators, Communication Arts, *Print* magazine, *How* magazine, and many Addy awards.

Sally's artwork has been included in several permanent collections, including Women Illustrators from the permanent collection of The Society of Illustrators. Her first children's book, *Brave Margaret*, was released in February 1999. Sally lives with her husband and two children in Annapolis, Maryland.

While the events, locations, and characters described in this book may be based on actual historical events and real people, this story is fictional.